THE ELIXIR FIXERS

SASHA AND PUCK
AND THE CURE FOR COURAGE

BOOK 3

DANIEL NAYERI

ILLUSTRATED BY ESTRELA LOURENÇO

Albert Whitman & Company
Chicago, Illinois

Library of Congress Cataloging-in-Publication data is on
file with the publisher.

First published in the United States of America
in 2019 by Albert Whitman & Company
ISBN 978-0-8075-7245-0 (hardcover)
ISBN 978-0-8075-7252-8 (ebook)

Printed in the United States of America
10 9 8 7 6 5 4 3 2 1 LB 24 23 22 21 20 19

Design by Ellen Kokontis

For more information about Albert Whitman & Company,
visit our website at www.albertwhitman.com

100 years of Albert Whitman & Company
Celebrate with us in 2019!

To Enchantment

MAP OF THE VILLAGE
SPARKSTONE MOUNTAINS
SUNDERDOWN FALLS
THE OLD TREE
A MYSTERIOUS PLACE
CATHEDRAL
GENTRY MANSION
SWELTERING RIVER
CAKER
MAYOR'S HOUSE
CHOCOLATE SHOP
GRANNY YENTA'S HOUSE
JEWELER
SHIVERING RIVER
THISTLEWOOD SWAMP
YULETIDE FESTIVAL
VILLAGE SQUARE
THE JUICY GIZZARD
MILLER
BAKER
COBBLER
VILLAGE GREEN
DOCKS
INN
BLACKSMITH
STABLES
STONE LAKE
WHISPERSHAW CASTLE

THE STORY SO FAR...

Sasha Bebbin lives in a village tucked away in a far-off corner of a world, between the mountains and the sea. She lives with her papa in an alchemy shop named the Juicy Gizzard. Her mother was the alchemist, but she has gone off to help fight against the Make Mad Order.

Now, Papa makes and sells the potions. But he's not a very good alchemist.

And Sasha, who doesn't even believe in magic, is worried that customers will start to complain. Then, Papa will be taken to the constable, who will give them a fine that they cannot afford to pay. And then, the wealthy gruel baron, Vadim Gentry, will buy up the Juicy Gizzard, and Sasha and Papa will be homeless.

And so, Sasha has her mission. Along with her sidekick, Puck—a mysterious wild boy from the woods—Sasha must use her detective skills to investigate the real reason every customer wants a potion—whether it's luck or love or just a cure for the hiccups. She has to do this without being discovered. And the hardest part? She has to find a way to make the potion come true, to give the customer the magic they were looking for, before anyone finds out!

CHAPTER 1

It was so cold that even the snow seemed to shiver as it fell quietly over the Village. In every window was a candle and a halo of frost. The animals huddled in their stables for warmth. The stablers huddled with them.

Far out on the outskirts of the Village, near the Willow Woods, sat an old stone cottage with a thatched roof. In front of the cottage, a rickety wooden sign half-covered in snow, dangled from a spike in the ground. It read: *The Juicy Gizzard Alchemy Shop: Makers of Fine Potions, Medicines, and Teas.*

Inside the cottage, the light was dim and bluish. It came from two star-shaped lanterns burning a white jelly. The candles were unlit. The fireplace was cold.

The shelves were overfull with bottles of every shape and type, filled with powders of different colors, liquids of various sliminess, and several vapors swirling in glass.

Papa Bebbin sat at a small desk in the corner of the shop, studying an open ledger. He squinted in the half-light, shook his head, and sighed.

"What?" said Sasha. She stood at the workbench, stirring liquid in a copper pot that sat on a small burner. The blue flame of the burner flickered its light over the ingredients on the counter.

"I'm sorry, what?" said Papa.

"I said, 'What?'" said Sasha.

"That's what I said," said Papa.

"You made a noise. I said, 'What?'"

"It's nothing to worry about," said Papa. Then he turned the page of the ledger and sighed again, this time as if a slab of stone had fallen on his chest.

"Ugga mugga," said Puck, rolling his eyes. He sat on the counter where Sasha was working, like a stray cat inviting himself to a dinner table.

"Puck's right," said Sasha. "Just tell us, and we'll worry less."

Papa considered it for a moment, then said, "It's nothing. Sorry."

There was a quiet moment. Papa read the ledger. Sasha stirred the pot.

Puck stole a cinnamon stick from Sasha's tray of ingredients and put it in his mouth. "You can't eat those," said Sasha.

Puck's cheeks stuck out, trying to hold the

entire cinnamon stick, but his eyes were wide as if to say, "Whatever do you mean?"

"I don't mean you *can't* as in you *shouldn't*," said Sasha. "I mean you *can't*."

Puck crunched on the cinnamon stick. He tried to keep his expression calm.

His face began to turn red. He chewed a few more times. He began to shake.

"I told you," said Sasha.

Puck tried to look innocent, but his eyes were watering.

"You can spit it out," said Sasha. "It's okay. I know you took it."

Puck spit out a glob of cinnamon and coughed and tried to scrape the taste of it from his tongue.

"Have some of this," said Sasha. She took her

ladle and poured some of the drink from the pot into a cup. Puck grabbed for it and drank it all in one gulp. He handed it back and panted for air.

Only after Sasha filled the cup again and gave it to him did she realize that she had been tricked.

"Wait," she said, "did you gag yourself on purpose?"

Puck shrugged, but his eyes twinkled as he took another gulp of her mulled honey drink.

"This is for Yuletide, you unmannered little burglar," said Sasha. "Get down."

She swiped him off the counter. The mulled honey had taken all morning to brew, and at each step, Puck had nosed in.

First, she had gathered a basketful of black-berries from the winter bush on the outskirts of the Willow Wood. Puck had stolen a handful and was caught purple-handed. Then Sasha cooked the blackberries in a pot with three cinnamon sticks and five stars of anise, which she had gotten as payment for cleaning out horse stalls for Oxiana the stabler.

Once the blackberries reduced down into a thick jam, she added the honey. She had gotten it from a wild beehive that Otto, their angry piglet, had dragged out of a hollow tree. Into the mixture, she added an orange pomander. She had gotten the orange from the fruit basket in the coolest corner of the basement. It was the last orange of the year, and almost too hard. She pushed clove buds into the rind in a lacy pattern. As it steeped in the liquid, the orange and clove would give off their flavors.

Then she added ten handfuls of newly fallen snow, which melted immediately in the steaming pot. She set it to a low simmer, and that was that. The family recipe for honey mull.

It was Mama's favorite tradition.

But this year, Sasha had to be the one to keep it going. She looked into the sweet, dark drink and saw a reflection of herself. It looked almost like her mother's face.

Sasha wondered where her mother was at that very moment.

Was she riding through the winter passes, across the mountains toward home? Was the war over? Or was she busy in some castle of the Knights of Daytime, crafting potions for the soldiers to fend off the hordes of shadows summoned by the Make Mad Order?

It comforted Sasha a little to think that if she couldn't be with her mother, at least they were both doing the same thing: staring into brewing pots.

Sasha filled a cup for Papa and walked over

to his desk. He was slumped over the ledger once again.

She already knew what was wrong. The new year was around the corner. At the end of Yuletide, after the winter festival, tax collectors would make their visit. If Sasha and Papa couldn't pay, the constable would make his visit, and soon they would be out of a home.

Sasha tapped Papa on the shoulder.

She tried to sound cheery. "It's officially Yuletide!" That was what Mama always said after the first sip of honey mull.

Papa sat up and took the cup. When he smiled, the lines around his eyes were deeper. He looked older than Sasha had ever seen him.

"Mmm," he said after he took a sip, "that is a perfect mixture, Sasha."

The drink seemed to perk him up. He shut the ledger with a thud.

"Is it bad?" said Sasha, nodding at the ledger.

"Yes," said Papa, pulling her into his arms. "It's bad. But your wonderful drink has cheered me up. It must have some happy magic in it." He took an eager gulp.

Sasha rolled her eyes. "No such thing as magic, Papa."

Her father coughed and spat theatrically. "No

magic? That's a funny thing for the daughter of alchemists to say."

Sasha shrugged. "And yet, I've said it."

"What an insult! What terrible naughtiness!"

He squeezed Sasha, and they both laughed.

"Now tell me what present you'd like for Yuletide. A new bracelet? A Bloomhoof pony?"

All Sasha really wanted was to know her mother was all right.

"Papa," said Sasha, "I'm not a kid anymore. Also, there are no such things as magic Bloomhoof ponies; otherwise I would want one." Also, she thought, Papa didn't have the money for gifts.

"What do you want for Yuletide?" said Sasha.

Papa took another drink of honey mull cider, breathed deeply, and said, "I want *two* ponies. And golden saddles for both. And peace throughout the world. And I want more bonbons than a mammoth could eat and a daughter whose brilliant mind will leave just a little room for the magic and mysterious. Oh, and ten more hugs daily. And I want everyone to call me Dearest and Wisest Papa." Then he held out his empty cup and said, "And I'd like another cup of magic juice, please."

Sasha laughed and took the cup. "Yes, Dearest and Wisest Papa. But it's not magic."

"Well, I don't care what you say," said Papa. "Your drink has given me hope that something good will come our way, and we'll have the money for taxes. So it must be magic."

Just then, they saw Puck from across the room, scrabbling up onto the counter toward the pot of honey mull. He had that look in his eyes like a rabid chipmunk in the middle of a chocolate shop. "Don't do it," said Sasha, but Puck wasn't listening. He reached into the pot and fished out the orange pomander.

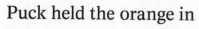

"You can't eat that," said Sasha.

Puck held the orange in both hands. He hesitated for only a moment.

"I'm telling you..." said Sasha.

But Puck stuffed the entire orange, and all the cloves, into his mouth and chomped on it with relish.

"Isn't he a curious thing?" wondered Papa.

For a few seconds, Puck smiled and kept chewing.

Papa and Sasha watched and waited.

Papa said, "I mean, isn't it proof of magic that a creature like him exists and hasn't died from eating something poisonous yet?"

When the spicy paste of orange peel and dried clove finally hit the back of Puck's throat, his eyes went wide, and he immediately stopped chewing. He made a tiny whimpering sound.

"You are extremely difficult, you know that?" said Sasha. "We warned you at least three times on this one. You're like some kind of uneducated trickster fairy or something."

Puck stood up straight, stiffened, and fell backward off the counter.

There was a thunderous crash.

The sound was much louder than Sasha expected.

A moment later, a huge sheet of snow slid off the roof and shook the whole house.

Bottles rattled on their shelves.

Papa jumped out of his chair.

Suddenly Sasha had forgotten all her frustration with the little guy and hoped only that he was all right. She ran around the counter.

"Puck! Are you okay? Puck!"

But when she came around the corner, she

saw that Puck had fallen onto a basket of puffy winter moss. He had spit out the orange and was smiling at his luck.

"But, wait," said Sasha, "if you didn't make that sound, where did it come from?"

Her answer came quickly. They heard the shouting of people outside.

For a second, Sasha wondered if the tax collectors had come early.

"Wait here," said Papa.

CHAPTER 2

Nobody waited. Sasha, Papa, and Puck all ran to the front door of the potion shop. When Papa opened the door, he was stopped by a pile of snow that had fallen from the roof.

But before Papa could suggest that they find some shovels, Puck ran headlong into the snow and plowed a little path.

Sasha and Papa followed.

They didn't have to go far. At the road, right in front of their shop, they saw a cart that had veered off and crashed into their wooden sign.

A pair of soldiers were standing in the ditch with their swords drawn. In front of them stood Otto—the Bebbins' family pig—growling. Otto was no bigger than a bread loaf, but the knights kept their distance.

"Back!" said one. "Back, you demon piglet."

Otto was furiously grunting, most likely because their cart was draped with an orange horse blanket, and Otto hated the color orange.

Papa shouted, "Otto, relent!" But Otto saw red when he saw orange, and paid no attention.

It was Puck who noticed the blanket first. He jumped onto the cart. The pair of soldiers seemed even more alarmed when they saw Sasha, Papa, and Puck.

"Take what you want, thieves," said one knight. "But know that we'll be sworn enemies after."

"Wait, we're not thieves," said Sasha.

"Then why did you run us off the road with your orc pig, and why is that gremlin rooting around in our stuff?"

"Oh. Oh!" said Sasha as the situation clarified in her mind. "We're not bandits at all. Puck is trying to help you."

Puck pulled the orange blanket into the cart and emerged. Otto stopped grumbling as soon as the blanket disappeared. "Everyone take a breath," said Papa. "Otto, if you go back to your pen, then there's an extra bit of dinner for you tonight."

Otto had nothing else to do, so he waddled back around the house toward his pen.

Suddenly, everyone felt a little silly. The knights put away their swords. Puck jumped from the cart and scrambled out of the ditch.

The cart had lost a wheel. The knights' horse was on the other side of the road, rummaging in the snow for a patch of grass to eat.

"Is this your house?" said one of the knights. He was tall and broad and seemed underdressed for the snow. The knight next to him looked identical, except that her boots, tunic, and helmet were green, and his were a peach color.

"What he means to say—now that we know you're not bandits—is we're sorry for the mess," the green knight said.

"Right," said the peach knight, "but if they don't live here, then we're sorry for something else. I was being precise."

"Like what? What would we be sorry for?"

"They could be customers. We should say sorry for blocking their exit."

The green knight scoffed. "They're not customers."

"You don't know," said the peach knight. "This is a shop. They could be customers."

"I know it's a shop," said the green knight.
"You drove right into their sign."

"Me?"

"Yeah, you."

"Me?"

"I said that already. You!"

"Are you two knights?" said Sasha.

"And more importantly, are you two related?"
said Papa.

"Brother and sister. How'd you guess?" said the peach knight.

Papa smiled and said, "You're dressed similar."

"That's cause we're hedge knights from Maraj," said the peach knight, standing up a bit straighter to show his uniform. "At the hedge knight academy, each knight is named after a color. I'm Coral, and she's Sage. We came for the Yuletide festival."

"Right," said Sage. "Heard there was a jousting tournament. Even heard a knight of the Kingdom of Daytime was coming."

Sasha perked up at the mention of a Daytime Knight.

"Really?" she said. "Does that mean the war is over?"

"'Fraid not," said Sage. "The knights will travel around sometimes, looking for heroes to recruit or going on secret missions."

Sasha's hope deflated. She said, "We should probably get you two out of there. The sun's going down."

Everyone agreed. Coral and Sage put their shoulders to the cart and pushed with all their might, but it didn't budge. Puck jumped into the ditch between them. He spit on his palms and rubbed them together, then he put his hands on the cart.

It was a funny picture, the little boy, barely up to their knees. But he seemed determined. So on the count of three, they all pushed. This time, the cart jumped out of the ditch and landed several feet beyond.

Sage petted Puck on the head and said, "Thanks, little guy."

Puck blushed and didn't know what to do, so he hugged her leg.

The hedge knights replaced the missing wheel,

lashed the cart to their horse, and went on their way. Sasha picked up the broken pieces of the sign and walked back toward the house.

Puck bounded up beside her. He was very pleased to have made new friends.

When they entered the shop, they saw Papa, revived with new excitement, rushing around, pulling different items from the shelves.

"Come in," he said. "We've got preparations to make, ho-ho!"

Sasha and Puck glanced at each other. Papa continued to bustle around. "I had the greatest idea. We could set up a market stall on the fairground and sell to all the people at the festival!"

Sasha's heart sank.

"Um, Papa. That's a lot of potions, and what about quality? Alchemy is a very delicate craft, you always say."

"I know," said Papa. "That's why we'll sell your delicious mulled honey."

"Regular mulled honey?" said Sasha.

"No. Delicious mulled honey."

"But no magic, right?"

"The magic of perfectly balanced flavors," said Papa.

"Yes, okay, but no magic ingredients?" said Sasha.

"The magic ingredient is love."

"Papa!" said Sasha.

"Okay, okay. No magic."

"It's a great idea," said Sasha.

"Guh! Guh!" said Puck. For the first time, Sasha felt all the tension release from her shoulders. It was a good plan. They could buy more supplies from the local greengrocer and still make enough gold to pay their taxes. And no one would ask for any potions. For a moment, everything was simple and easy.

Then the door of the shop slammed open, and a man came running in. "Mister Bebbin," he said, "I need your help."

It was Sergeant Latouche. His coat was clean and well pressed. His mustache was thin and sharp, like his nose. He was a handsome man. And he came from a family of soldiers. He was too brittle to have ever been a soldier, but he had the title of sergeant.

"Come in, Sergeant Latouche. Would you like some cider?" said Papa.

Latouche shook his head. "No, no, I need a potion," he said. "A magical one."

Sasha was growing nervous. But she knew that Latouche was a wealthy man with a good life. So he couldn't possibly want anything *too* magical.

"In fact," said Latouche, "I need a potion more magical and wondrous than anything you've made in your life!"

Uh-oh, thought Sasha.

"All right," said Papa. "Just tell me what you want the magic potion to do."

Sasha hoped it wasn't something too impossible.

"I want to become the bravest in the world, even braver than the knights from the Kingdom of Daytime," said Latouche.

Sasha nearly fainted.

CHAPTER 3

The Wander Inn was cozy, joyful, and loud.

Even though it was already a dark winter night, all the windows shone brightly. At the center of the back wall sat a fireplace. The fire roared under a black cauldron. A rabbit stew bubbled in the cauldron.

The smell filled the air and made Sasha's belly warble. She sat in a booth near the door, with Sergeant Latouche. The rest of the inn was taken up by dozens of soldiers, knights, squires, and merchants, all visiting the Village to attend

the festival the next day.

The innkeeper, Uncle Nestor, was a barrel-shaped man with a bushy red mustache. He stood behind the oak bar, serving cider to the guests, laughing at their jokes, and bellowing orders if any of them got too rowdy. His daughter, Mina, had red hair like her father's, in a big bun on top of her head. She ran from table to table serving bowls of stew. The place was so busy that she hadn't gotten to Sasha yet.

Sasha was a detective and a scientist. She was there on a mission. She was also hungry. But she tried her best to observe as much as possible. The first thing she noticed was that everyone was a little nervous. It was the night before the jousting tournament, so a lot of the soldiers seemed to have that on their minds.

A group of them were passing the time with a game of dice. When one knight turned over his cup and revealed all ones on the dice, he got a panicked look on his face. It was apparently a very unlucky result. He immediately put one hand  over his right eye and spit into the dice cup. It must have been a superstition to ward off bad luck, Sasha thought.

At the bar, a couple of soldiers kept asking Uncle Nestor for advice. This made Sasha guess that he had been a great warrior once upon a time.

On the wall behind him hung a row of portraits. Sasha wondered what they were. She nudged Latouche and said, "What are those pictures, do you suppose?"

Sasha had followed Latouche to the Wander Inn after he had purchased his potion. He was so distracted that he hardly noticed.

Her question snapped Latouche out of his troubled thoughts. "Huh? Are you still following me? Where are your parents?"

Sasha ignored his question.

"The paintings. Do you know about them?"

"Oh, that's Nestor's wall of bravery and knavery."

"Sounds silly," said Sasha.

"That's because you're a child and there are no pictures of candy."

Sasha was annoyed but let him continue.

"The wall of bravery is for the greatest heroes of our village. Remember when that wild boar was menacing the Willow Wood and attacking travelers?"

"No," said Sasha, even though the description sounded a lot like Otto.

"That's because you weren't born yet, but it was a big deal. The miller's son, Khabib, wrestled

the boar into a cage and
saved everybody. So Nestor
asked Mina to paint him.
That's him up there with
the scar on his face."

Latouche described other
heroic deeds that got people onto the wall. Each
time, Mina had painted their portrait.

Sasha asked, "And what about knavery?"

"Nestor loves a good joke," said Latouche.
"That's why they called him the Laughing
Knight. One time, the milkmaid painted a
spider on the bottom of the tax collector's cup,
and when he saw it, he spilled all over himself
and fell off his stool. Nestor laughed for a week.
That's the milkmaid's picture up there, with the
spider on her shoulder."

Latouche went silent again as he lost himself
in the stories of the heroes on the wall. Sasha

watched as Puck ran back and forth from the bar to Mina, getting her cups and towels or whatever she needed. It seemed that he was friends with Uncle Nestor, who tousled his hair every time he ran under the counter to get Mina another bowl of radishes or rye bread.

Sasha wondered how they knew each other. She still knew so little about Puck. He would disappear sometimes. She'd find him asleep a few days later, curled up by the back door of their house, as if nothing had happened.

When Sage the hedge knight reached for a mug of cider and accidentally toppled it, Puck scampered to the spill almost before it hit the floor. A piece of the mug broke off, so Sage made the knightly salute—one hand over her right eye—and spat into the fireplace.

Her brother, Coral, did it, too, as extra insurance against bad luck.

Latouche sighed as he pulled the cork off the glass bottle he'd bought from Papa Bebbin.

"So I just drink it, and it's magic?" he said.

Sasha didn't believe in magic.

"That's what it says on the label," she said.

Latouche tipped the bottle and drank it all in one gulp. His face turned red. That was probably from the volcano peppers Papa liked to use. Sasha waited as Latouche coughed, guzzled his cup of cider, coughed some more, then fixed his hair. Sasha thought Latouche was distracted enough, so she decided the best thing to do would be to come right out and ask what she wanted to know. She said, "Why would you want a bravery potion, anyway?"

"That's a good question," said Latouche.

"What's the answer?"

"The answer is that I'm not going to answer that."

Sasha wasn't getting anywhere. Thankfully, Mina appeared with their bowls of stew. She set them down quickly but gently, so none of it sloshed onto the oak table. She put a hand on Latouche's shoulder and said, "Sorry for the wait. Can I get you anything else?"

Mina smiled at Sasha, and Sasha noticed splotches of food and paint all over her apron. If Sasha could have had an older sister, she thought Mina would have been a good one. Anybody who was kind to Puck was probably a good person. For a moment, Sasha thought, *Is he trying to be brave in order to talk to Mina?*

But that seemed unlikely. The last time Sasha had seen Latouche, he was wooing the local chocolatier, Ms. Kozlow, and he hadn't been shy at all.

"Packed house tonight," Latouche said, looking up at Mina. "Are you going to the festival tournament?"

"Probably not," said Mina.

"Okay," said Latouche.

His tone didn't sound like horrible disappointment. Sasha decided that Latouche was probably not in love with Mina.

A roar of cheers came from a table in the far corner of the inn, where several knights were arm-wrestling. A tall soldier with a missing tooth, long, greasy black hair, and mean eyes had won again.

Uncle Nestor scowled whenever he looked at the arm-wrestling knights.

Mina rolled her eyes.

Sasha watched as Puck scooted up to the table, under the winning soldier's arm, to take a few of the empty glasses back to the kitchen. But the soldier turned at the wrong moment, bumped into Puck, and leaped back as if he'd seen a spider.

"Oy! What're you?"

Puck didn't seem to understand. He said, "Guh," and reached for the soldier's cup. The soldier pulled the cup out of Puck's reach and said, "You some kind of black cat?"

The others at the table laughed. Puck was almost always covered in dirt, and he did look a little like a cat if you weren't paying attention.

The room was suddenly quiet. Everyone had stopped their conversations to watch. From behind the bar, Uncle Nestor growled a warning. "Scolario..."

Someone in the crowd whispered, "That's Scolario the Bad Hander."

But Scolario didn't pay attention.

He said, "A black cat's bad luck." Then he made the knight's salute and spat right on Puck's head.

Sasha slammed her palms on the table and stood up. "Hey!" she said. But no one noticed. Puck stood in front of Scolario with his tiny hands balled into fists. He was barely bigger than Scolario's boot. His eyes were angry slits. His whole body shook.

Scolario laughed and turned back in his seat.

Sasha started to squeeze out of the booth to rush to Puck's aid. But it was too late.

Puck gnashed his teeth like a baby bear, then let out a roar as he leapt at Scolario's face. He had to grab the knight's greasy hair to climb up his shoulders, but Puck was very nimble when he wanted to be.

"Oy!" said Scolario in surprise.

All the soldiers at the table jumped up and began to shout at once. Puck held on to Scolario's hair with both hands and began to head-butt the man in a wild flurry.

It only worked for a moment. Scolario reached back and grabbed Puck by the neck and wrenched him around. Sasha was about to scream.

Just then, the door of the inn flew open, and a deep, commanding voice said, "Enough!"

Everyone turned.

In the doorway stood a knight who was thicker, wider, and taller than the door itself. In the silence, Sasha could hear Coral leaning over to his sister to say, "Who's that?"

"Belfort," said Scolario with a sneer.

The man named Belfort had a thick yellow beard, cut straight at the chin like a row of wheat. On his chest, he wore the crest of the Knights of the Kingdom of Daytime.

"Put the creature down," said Belfort.

"And what if I don't?" said Scolario. But he put Puck down as he said it.

The two knights stared at each other. Finally, Scolario spat on the floor and sat down, grumbling. Belfort didn't have anything else to say, so he approached Uncle Nestor and greeted him. The crowd slowly began to resume their conversations.

Puck ran to Mina and hugged her leg. She didn't seem bothered by how dirty he was. She picked him up—even though he made more smudges on her apron—and whispered nice things to him.

Sasha was still trembling. When she sat back down to finish her stew, Latouche said, "See that? That's why I bought the potion." He nodded at Belfort the knight.

"You want to be like Belfort?"

"Who wouldn't?" said Latouche. "Look at him.

Magic or no magic, everybody in here knows that he's not afraid of anything. I want that."

Sasha nodded. She had what she'd come for.

Latouche wanted to be just like Belfort the knight.

Sasha wondered what Latouche could possibly do to be more brave.

Then she remembered.

Sasha dropped her spoon into her bowl.

"Wait a minute," she said. "Are you planning to enter the tournament of knights?"

"Yes," said Latouche.

"You can't," said Sasha.

"I can."

"Just so everyone will know you're brave?"

"The bravest," said Latouche as he flicked the empty potion bottle onto the table.

"I was afraid you'd say that," said Sasha.

CHAPTER 4

Sasha stepped out into the wintry night, shivered, and pulled her hood over her head. It was quiet. She was alone.

Back inside the Wander Inn, the knights and merchants laughed and told stories. Puck stayed to help Mina and Uncle Nestor. Latouche sat at his table, wondering when his magic bravery potion would kick in. The good knight Belfort and the villain Scolario sat at their tables and enjoyed their dinners.

Outside, the snow had made a white carpet

seen from outside was coming from behind a post at the far end of the stables. Horses and mules huddled in their stalls, trying to find some sleep.

As Sasha approached the faint light, she was suddenly struck by the idea that maybe she was unwelcome.

Right then, she heard an angry voice. "What do you mean, you don't know?"

Sasha knew the voice. As she stepped into the edge of the light, she saw Vadim Gentry, the gruel baron. He was the one wearing the fancy shoes. He stood over an older man, hunched in the shape of a lump. It was Gorch, the village lamplighter.

Sasha gasped at the sight of them.

She leaped backward, out of the light.

"What was that?" said Vadim, twisting around to see behind him. Gorch made a low grumbling

sound and lifted the lamp in that direction.

Sasha dove to the floor to avoid being seen. She crawled on her hands and knees into the nearest horse stall.

Inside the stall, a nervous horse snorted at her. *Please, please, please don't stomp me*, thought Sasha. Thankfully, the horse moved away. Sasha crawled into the far corner and tried to breathe quietly.

She heard Vadim say, "Dumb animals. Probably saw a mouse."

Sasha leaned down and peeked through a hole in the slats on the side of the stall.

Gorch lumbered on his good leg. The other was a wooden peg. Gorch's job was to keep the lamps in the Village full of oil, and light them when the sun went down. In the mornings, he would snuff them out. Some people said he lost his leg when he was a pirate on the King Sea, but no one ever asked.

His teeth were missing or black. His smell was sour.

Sasha couldn't imagine why Vadim Gentry, the richest man in all the valley, would ever want to meet with Gorch. But Sasha also knew that Vadim was a greedy man. And greed made people do odd things.

Gorch searched the pockets of his tattered coat and finally came up with a scrap of paper. "Urm. Here," he grumbled. "Urm. Here it is. I wrote it. Hold on. Urm. I wrote it down."

He unwrinkled the paper and squinted to read. "Here it is. First round. Latouche goes against Volkov. Urm. And Belfort fights some hedge knight by the name of Sage. And Bad Hander's got one named Coral."

"There," said Vadim. "Coral. Find me his horse."

"Urm. Hold on."

Gorch limped toward the first stall, where Sasha was hiding, and squinted into the darkness. Sasha tried to make herself as small as possible.

Please don't be this one. Please don't be this one.

Gorch turned away with a grunt and looked at the next stall. Sasha breathed out a sigh as quietly as she could.

"This one."

Vadim nudged Gorch aside and said, "Good. I'll do it myself."

Sasha could hear the sounds of a knife cutting into leather. She wished she could be sure of what they were doing, but it was too dangerous to look.

When the horse made a sudden neighing, Sasha gasped by accident. Vadim twirled around once again and seemed to look right at her through the crack in the stall door.

Sasha pulled away from the light.

She was certain that he had seen her this time.

For a moment, everyone held their breath.

Sasha's arms shook with cold and fear. She closed her eyes and tried to be more still than she had ever been before.

"Come on," said Vadim. "We've secured our bet."

The two men walked out of the stables. Gorch put out his lamp so no one would see them leaving the stable.

Sasha waited till she was certain they were gone. Then she gasped for air.

Her teeth began to chatter.

As she left, she patted the horse in her stall and said, "Thank you for not kicking me. I pray your children will be Bloomhoof stallions."

The horse knocked into her with his muzzle as if to say she was welcome.

Sasha snuck out of the stables and ran all the way home.

She had just heard Vadim Gentry cheat to help Scolario the Bad Hander in the knights' tournament. But who could she tell?

And if she did tell, what would Vadim do? He had always schemed to buy the shop from Papa, but would he double his efforts if he knew Sasha had caught him?

As Sasha went to bed that night, she wondered if she had gotten herself into more trouble than she could possibly handle.

CHAPTER 5

The next morning, Puck refused to wake up after a long night of helping Mina at the inn, so Sasha and Papa loaded their wheelbarrow and pushed it all the way to the village green. Merchants, peddlers, tinkers, and cooks were all setting up their stands to sell their goods at the festival. At the center of the field were the tournament grounds, where the knights would joust.

It's going to be a rough day, thought Sasha, as they lifted a giant rock of sugar and set it on the counter.

"It's going to be a great day!" said Papa as he began to assemble his scales.

Sasha got to work making the recipe. She mixed the spices in a round pot over a low fire. She found a snowbank that looked untouched from the night before and scooped ten handfuls into the pot. As she stirred, Sasha pulled her cloak tight to protect against the wind.

The cloak was a gift from her mother.

Everything seemed to remind Sasha of her mother—the holiday festival, the mulled cider, even the smell of fried dough rolled in cinnamon, wafting from the cinnamon man's tent. Mama loved all those things. Sasha tried not to think about it.

When the cider was ready, she lifted the pot and poured it into a samovar to keep it warm. Then she started a new batch.

She worried they wouldn't sell enough cider.

She worried they wouldn't have enough money for taxes.

She worried that Mama would never come back.

She worried that Latouche would demand a refund and cause a stink if he lost the tournament.

"Come one, come all!" shouted the green-grocer, who was also the village herald whenever there was news, because he had the loudest voice and biggest personality. He stood on a turnip crate and cupped his hands around his mouth. "The tournament of knights is about to begin!"

People were starting to fill the market. Sasha

and Papa already had a few customers. For each one, Papa weighed a lump of sugar, dropped it into a cup, and handed the cup to Sasha.

She poured the cider from the samovar and received a coin as she handed out the drink. She was distracted the whole time, looking at the tournament field. Sasha knew she didn't have the time to spend all day pouring honey mull cider, not if she was going to help Latouche find his bravery.

"First up," shouted the greengrocer, "Scolario the Bad Hander against the Coral Knight."

No one cheered for Scolario. Sasha heard Coral's sister, Sage, shouting from the stands, "You get 'em, Coral. Knock that goon from his horse!"

Sasha strained to see through the crowd.

The two knights mounted their horses and grabbed their jousting spears.

The crowd from the night before stood beside Sasha's cider stand and made their bets. "Who you got?" said a bearded soldier.

"That coral knight's pretty stout. I says he wins."

"Yarp," said another. "Wouldn't wanna cross paths with Bad Hander in a dark alley, or nuffin. But he ain't no joust type."

As Bad Hander and Coral rode their horses to the starting positions, the whole fair seemed to turn and look. Only Papa was uninterested.

The greengrocer raised the flag in the air.

Bad Hander's horse made an angry snort.

Coral sat in his saddle. He looked noble.

The grocer dropped the flag, and both men spurred their horses into a gallop. Their flat-tipped spears were pointed at each other.

Sasha noticed a leather strap dangling loose on Coral's saddle. And suddenly, she knew

exactly what was
about to happen.

"Coral's going to
fall," said Sasha.

And at that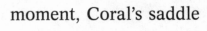
moment, Coral's saddle
slipped to the side, and he fell off his horse.

The crowd gasped in shock that such a
strapping knight would tumble from his horse.
Coral landed in the mud.

Bad Hander rode past.

Gorch and Vadim Gentry both cheered from
their seats.

A soldier from the night before turned around
and looked at Sasha. "How'd you know he was
gonna fall?"

"Who, me?" said Sasha.

"Yeah, you. You said he was gonna fall, and
he fell."

Of course, Sasha knew it was because she had heard Gorch and Vadim cut the saddle straps the night before. But the small crowd of soldiers didn't know that. She could tell they were a little scared. "Maybe she's got magic," said one soldier. Everyone stepped away from the cider stand. One made the knight's salute and spit into his cup.

Sasha started to protest, but then she saw Latouche sitting in the stands with a mopey expression on his face, waiting for his turn. At that moment, Sasha had her plan to save him.

She turned to the soldiers with a smile and said, "That's right. I'm kinda magic."

One of the soldiers fainted and fell back into a pile of snow.

CHAPTER 6

"Papa, I gotta go," said Sasha.

"You can't," said Papa.

"But I have something very important to do."

"Understood."

"So I can go?"

"Of course not. What could be more important that this?" Papa gestured at the samovar of cider, the block of sugar, and the line of customers. "We've just begun to make some coin," he said, "and we've got taxes and bills—don't forget."

"I didn't forget," said Sasha. As far as she was

concerned, her plan to help Latouche in the tournament was most important because it would prove their potion was magic and keep their shop out of trouble.

Papa handed her a cup without even looking. They were so busy that Sasha hardly had time to complain.

She poured cider into the cup. She handed it to a young woman wearing a long fur coat, then said, "Thank you," and took the woman's coin. In her mind, Sasha fretted about what to do. Latouche had already gone to the stables to get his horse ready. She was running out of time.

When she turned around to grab another cinnamon stick to stir with, she saw Puck standing right beside her, as if he appeared by magic.

Of course, it wasn't magic, thought Sasha.

It was just a coincidence.

"Of all the odds and oddity," she said, "where have you been?"

Puck yawned and scratched his head. His eyes were still droopy from sleep.

"While you were napping, we had about three emergencies."

"Guh," said Puck.

"No, I will not give you cider." But as soon as she said it, an obvious idea occurred to her. "Actually," she said, leaning down to whisper. "Actually, you can have some cider."

"Guh!" said Puck.

"With extra sugar. But you have to stand here and do my job so I can take care of something."

"Guh! Guh!" said Puck, excited to help, or maybe just to drink extra cider. He tried to push past her to get started, but Sasha stuck her palm out.

"Wait," she said, "not yet. Do you understand what to do?"

Puck seemed insulted. He gestured that he'd take the cup and pour the cider. He rolled his eyes as he did it.

"Wrong," said Sasha. "The important part is the coin. You have to remember to take the coin. And you can't lose them."

"Guh. Guh," said Puck.

"So you'll take the coins, then?"

"Guuuuuuuh."

"And you'll put them in the safe box."

"Guh!"

"And you won't drink from the cups before you hand them out."

Puck just sighed.

"And you stir with this cinnamon stick. Not your hand. Not your feet."

Puck gave her a look.

"Fine. Okay. I trust you. Thank you," said Sasha.

Puck nodded and jumped onto a stool to take up his position. Sasha waited for a particularly long line of customers, and then she snuck off. Papa was happy chatting with people, chiseling lumps of sugar. He handed cups back to Puck and didn't bother looking over.

Sasha hoped it would stay that way until she returned. She pulled the hood of her mother's cloak over her head. She grabbed a cup of cider,

covered it with the hem of her cloak so it wouldn't spill, and dashed across the fairground. As she weaved between the kebab stands and carnival games, she reviewed her plan. If she had the time, she would have written it in her detective's notebook.

First, her problem: Latouche wanted to win the knights' tournament to show off his bravery, but Latouche wasn't a knight. And there was no way he was going to out-joust the real knights on his own.

Then she would list her resources, like "pluck," which she certainly had. She was very plucky. And "Puck," who was a very useful creature for climbing things and biting other things. And lastly, she would write in big letters, "BAD LUCK," because the soldiers all seemed terrified by it.

At the inn, when the soldier had rolled snake eyes, he had immediately made the knight's salute and spat in his hand. It seemed the soldier believed that in order to ward off bad luck he had to salute and spit on the source of the luck. So he spat in his hand because he had thrown the dice.

Then, after the cup broke, the other soldier had spit in the fire—where clay pottery was made. And when Bad Hander had called Puck a black cat, he'd spit on Puck's head.

Of course, Sasha didn't believe such silly superstitions. But the information was a powerful tool she could use. With pluck, Puck, and bad luck, Sasha had everything she needed to execute her plan.

"Hiya, Mister Latouche!" said Sasha. Before he could answer, she added, "You look great up there. Very heroic. Unstoppable. Not nervous at all. Supercapable...and strong...and handsome."

Latouche snapped out of his worrying. "Huh? Oh, yes. I'm fine. They should be calling us any moment." As he spoke, Sasha barely paid attention. She was busy checking the harnesses on Latouche's saddle. She inspected every strap to make sure Vadim Gentry hadn't cut them.

"Great!" said Sasha. "I'm sure you'll be great."

Then she ran off to find his opponent.

She crossed the snowy field, still holding the cider with two hands. On the other side was one of Bad Hander's friends. She had tiger stripes painted on her face and long braids. Her armor was covered in spikes. Her helmet was shaped like a tiger head. Her horse was also armored and looked mad enough to charge through a castle wall. Its giant hooves clopped on the cobblestone like giant hammers.

When Sasha arrived, the knight was shouting at her squire. "No, not that one, the other one!"

The squire grabbed at a different jousting spear and looked up at the knight, who snorted like an angry dragon. The squire quickly grabbed another. This one seemed to be the right one, because the knight had nothing mean to say about it.

As she snatched the spear away from the squire, the knight said, "And where's that village goon? What's his name? Gorch. Tell that Gorch I don't like the hay he's feeding Daisy."

Sasha decided she had better present herself before Gorch arrived. She approached the terrifying warhorse and said to the knight, "Hello, I'm Sasha."

"Get outta my way," said the knight.

That hadn't worked. Sasha tried another approach. "Is your warhorse really named Daisy?"

"It stands for Deadly Apocalypse Is Surely Yours, why?"

"Oh. Wow. Okay, that is very aggressive," said Sasha. The greengrocer had already begun to call the audience to begin the joust. Sasha had to hurry.

"I just wanted to say good luck."

"Okay, you said it," said the knight.

"And I wanted to give you this cider. It's for good luck too."

The knight considered it. Then she put out her spiky glove. "Fine. Give it."

Sasha bounded up to give her the cup. But just as the knight touched it, Sasha tripped, and the cup fell from both their hands. It landed on the cobblestone and shattered. The squire, the

knight, even Daisy, all seemed to gasp at once.

The knight sat up straight. She put one hand to her eye and looked around for a fire to spit into, but there wasn't one close by. She spat toward Sasha instead and said, "You clumsy fool."

The greengrocer finished calling their names. The joust had begun.

"Well," said Sasha, "good luck!"

She jumped out of the warhorse's path and watched as the knight began the competition. The knight seemed distracted, and when she met Latouche in the middle of the green, he managed to graze his spear off her shoulder. She fell to the ground with a thud and a curse.

Latouche also fell—he'd lost his balance—but that was after he cleared the field, so he won.

Sasha ran up to him. "Are you okay?"

She tried to help him up, but he pulled away.

"Yes. Fine. Thank you." He was embarrassed because everyone was laughing at the double knockdown.

"You seemed really confident out there," said Sasha.

"I did?"

"You did."

"Well, I felt terrified."

Latouche walked his horse back to the stables. Sasha was tempted to follow him and give encouragement, but the odds were that Papa had already noticed she was gone. "Crumbsy bumsy," she said to herself. "If only he hadn't fallen from his horse."

Her plan to make Latouche feel brave had only sort of worked. She had a lot more to do if Latouche was going to win the tournament. In the meantime, she ran back to the cider stand, hoping she could sneak in.

But when Sasha arrived, the stand was empty, except for Puck sitting on the counter with his feet dangling, and Papa with his arms crossed and his mustache in the angry position.

"Uh-oh," said Sasha.

She was caught.

CHAPTER 7

"I know you're mad," said Sasha as she walked behind the counter to busy herself. "And you're right to be mad, but I just want to say I only left for a couple minutes, and I made sure Puck could handle it, and I ran right back."

She scooped handfuls of snow into the pot to melt. Papa remained silent. Sasha poured a basket of blackberries into the pot and began to measure the spices. She glanced at him. He was still watching and waiting.

"What?" said Sasha.

"You know what," said Papa.

"Okay, I'm sorry."

"Sorry for what?"

"For running off. For not being responsible. I don't know."

Papa sighed. "You knew I needed you here."

"Right, yes. I'm sorry."

Papa helped Puck get down from the counter. He said, "Puck has a lot of wonderful qualities, but we needed you. He forgot to take coins from half the customers, and he spilled cider on the other half."

"I understand," said Sasha.

"But that's not the worst of it."

"Oh crumbsy. He didn't bite anybody, did he? You didn't bite anyone, did you?"

Puck shook his head. His eyes were big and innocent.

Papa said, "No, Sasha, the worst part is that

you disobeyed me. I trusted that you heard me when I told you I needed you here."

For the first time, Sasha was truly sorry. She was so worried about her plan to help Latouche that she had betrayed Papa's trust. She stopped stirring the blackberries and said, "I'm really sorry."

"If we can't trust each other..." said Papa.

"I know. I know." Sasha didn't want to think about it—the fact that her mother was off somewhere, and all they had in this world was each other.

"I'm going to buy more blackberries," said Papa. "Would you promise me you'll stay here?"

"Yes. Sure."

Papa turned and walked into the holiday market.

Sasha kicked at a pile of snow. "This holiday is the worst."

"And you," said Sasha, "why didn't you collect money for the drinks?"

Puck shrugged.

"Do you even know what money is?" said Sasha.

Puck shrugged again.

"Okay, well, the odds are that you'll completely bungle this, but I'm stuck here, so I need you to help with the next part of my plan."

Puck made a happy grunt and ran around the counter to hear what Sasha needed him to do.

A few moments later, Puck was running off toward the tournament field, giggling as Sasha watched from the stand. Puck was perfect for this part of the plan because Latouche's next opponent was none other than Scolario the Bad Hander. And Sasha already knew that Scolario thought black cats were bad luck.

Puck, who probably hadn't bathed in his entire

life, was still covered in dirt. So when he scurried in front of Bad Hander on all fours and dove under a wagon cart, Scolario was certain it was a cat.

Even though Sasha couldn't hear Scolario from afar, she could tell he shouted a curse at his attendant and spat on the ground. But it was no use; the cat was gone. The bad luck was set. Scolario looked furious as he stalked off to get his horse.

Sasha cheered as she stirred the new pot of cider. She was beginning to think her plan just might work after all. But her celebration was short-lived, because at that moment she saw the last person on earth she wanted to see, walking straight toward her cider stand.

CHAPTER 8

It was Vadim Gentry, the man who was cheating to win the knights' tournament, the richest baron in the Village, and the one who was trying to take their shop.

He was a large man with a trim mustache. He wore a deep-red overcoat with lots of buttons and buckles. He loomed over the counter. Sasha felt very uncomfortable. Not knowing what else to do, she said, "Would you like a cider?"

"Very well," said Vadim.

Sasha used the chisel to break off a chunk

of sugar. As she did, she was relieved to see Puck return from his mission. He climbed on the counter and played with a stack of cups. He kept his eyes on Vadim.

Sasha wondered what the baron wanted. She poured the hot cider from the samovar and watched the sugar dissolve in the amber-colored drink. She held out the cup.

"You know what is odd?" said Vadim, taking the cup and reaching into his pocket for a coin. "I was in the stables last night when I heard a little scurrying creature. All by itself. I thought, it must be a rat. Any other creature would have the sense to be home with its parents at that time of night—away from the cold. Away from dangers. Wouldn't you think?"

Puck jumped up on his haunches and growled softly. He knew that Vadim was making veiled threats. Sasha didn't know what to do. Her cheeks must have been red, but she tried to act calm. She shrugged and said, "I don't know. That will be one coin, please."

Vadim held out the coin. When Sasha reached for it, he pulled it back. "Well, if it was a rat in those stables, I suppose it would run away and never return."

Puck growled again, but Sasha put a hand on his shoulder to keep him from jumping. She tried to keep from trembling and repeated herself. "That will be one coin, please."

Finally, Vadim gave her the coin. But as he did, he looked into her eyes and said, "I don't like rats, do you?"

Puck was ready to pounce, but a great, booming voice interrupted them. "Nobody likes rats," said Belfort the knight, who had approached from the market. "But if we hurt every creature smaller than ourselves, then you

could be mean to this little girl, and I could be very mean to you. Wouldn't you say, Baron?"

Vadim Gentry seemed to shrink in the presence of Belfort. But Sasha was overjoyed to see the Daytime Knight suddenly appear.

"Of course," said Vadim. "Yuletide is a holiday for peace, after all." With that, the baron turned and walked away. Sasha breathed a sigh of relief.

Vadim knew it had been her in the stables. Belfort had arrived just in time. "Thank you," she said. She began to make another cup of cider to give to him. Belfort chuckled. He held

his giant hand out to Puck, and Puck jumped onto it. Belfort lifted Puck up onto his shoulder. "I like your friend," said Belfort. Puck looked around the winter fair from his new perch on Belfort's shoulder. He giggled with the delight of being so tall and made grunty noises to himself.

Belfort laughed, then turned to Sasha and said, "You're Maxima's daughter."

Sasha stopped chiseling the sugar stone and looked up. She hadn't heard her mother's name in a while.

"Yeah. Yes, sir. How did you know?"

"You have her…intensity. And she talks about you all the time."

"You've talked to my mom? Recently? When? Where?" said Sasha.

"That's the intensity I mean," said Belfort. "I fought alongside her unit last season. We protected a caravan from the Make Mad raiders. She's very good, you know."

"I know," said Sasha.

"And she talks about you constantly."

That, Sasha didn't know.

"I was stationed to guard her lab. All night, she would mix potions and tell me how clever you are."

"That sounds like her," said Sasha.

She handed a cup to Belfort. "No charge," she said.

"Thank you," said Belfort. He took a sip through his mustache.

"You know," he said, "I have a girl your age. Unlike you, she solves all her problems with her hands instead of her mind. You'd make a good team."

Behind them, the grocer had once again taken his post. "In this next round..." he shouted, "Scolario the Bad Hander versus our very own Sergeant Latouche!" A scatter of applause went up for Latouche. Everyone must have been surprised that he even made it to the second stage of the knights' tournament.

But Sasha was still thinking about her mom and the war. She just wanted it all to end and for her mother to return.

"I'm like you," said Belfort. "I just want it all to end too." He said the second part in a whisper, as if he could read her mind.
He explained. "I can tell by your expression. I'm terrified every day that I won't see my Lily again."

Puck made a grunt like, "No way...you?" And Sasha said as much. "Really? You're scared?"

It was so hard to imagine Belfort, the man of stone, the Daytime Knight, scared of anything. He nodded. "Of course I'm scared. If you're not scared, you don't understand the dangers in a situation. If you're clever, and I know you're very clever, you see all the things that can go wrong."

Sasha had never thought of fear as a mark of intelligence.

"It's okay to be scared," said Belfort. "Your job is to face the fear."

Puck sat on Belfort's shoulder and stared at the side of his face with a mixture of wonder and admiration.

On the knights' field, Scolario and Latouche took up their spears and trotted their horses to the starting lines. The greengrocer had taken the moment to tell everyone about his prices for fresh turnips. Finally, he said, "Ready...begin!"

Scolario looked shaky from the start. His charger dashed forward, but he pulled the reins back and confused the horse. They both seemed nervous. Latouche rode high in his saddle, almost standing up, and pushed the jousting spear into Scolario's shoulder. If Scolario had been in position, leaning forward, it would have glanced off him. But Bad Hander was sitting back, so Latouche pushed him all the way off his horse. Scolario hit the ground with a clang of metal. The crowd erupted in applause.

Latouche rode past and circled around.

He didn't even wave to the crowd. He was shaking his head as if he was upset.

Of all the odds and oddity, thought Sasha, *why is he* still *upset?* Her plan had worked. Puck had been the perfect black cat to bring bad luck to Bad Hander. But Latouche still seemed unsatisfied. She had to find out why before he found a reason to blame Papa's potion. Sasha knew that Papa would be upset. But if Latouche complained, they might have to pay a fine, or they might lose customers. And either way, they wouldn't be able to pay their taxes. And if that happened, Baron Gentry was just waiting to pounce on them and steal their shop.

Sasha wiped her hands on a towel and ducked under the counter.

"I'm sorry, Mister Belfort," she said as she ran toward the knights' field. "Something's come up!"

Puck watched her go and made a grunty noise. He turned and kissed Belfort on the cheek, then hugged his head as hard as he could. After that, Puck scrambled down the knight's arm and ran after Sasha, shouting, "Gooby, gooby, gooby!"

CHAPTER 9

Sasha caught up with Latouche just as he was dismounting his horse and taking off his helmet. She followed him into the stables. "That was amazing!" she said, running up beside him. "Only the bravest could face Scolario."

"Guh!" said Puck, reenacting the spear thrust and making action sounds.

But Latouche tossed his helmet aside and led his horse back to its stable without an answer. Sasha followed.

On the far side of the field, Sasha could see

that Scolario was shouting curses and looking for the black cat that had caused him to doubt himself.

As Latouche gave his horse some feed, he sighed and said, "I don't know. I was trembling the whole time."

"We couldn't tell," said Sasha.

"Yeah, but it wasn't special. People see

bravery, and they marvel at it. They tell stories about it. Who cares if I knocked over a distracted goon? Nobody."

Sasha felt the frustration well up.

She and Puck had been running back and forth in the holiday market all day. She had worked at their stall as hard as she could, and Papa was probably furious that she had disappeared again. She had exhausted herself arranging everything so Latouche would feel brave. And still—still!—he complained.

Sasha wanted to cry. But she didn't want anyone to see her. She didn't want anyone to think she was a baby.

Suddenly, the answer struck her.

All this time, she thought Latouche wanted to *feel* a certain way. But every time he complained, it wasn't about *being* brave. It was about being *seen* being brave.

He wanted to impress someone. But who?

Sasha watched as Latouche glanced at the stands. He was looking for someone.

Could it be Mina, the innkeeper's daughter? No.

Sasha remembered her conversation with Latouche back at the Wander Inn, when he told her about Uncle Nestor's wall of bravery and knavery. Suddenly, it was so obvious. Latouche wanted Uncle Nestor to see him being brave.

"Of course," said Sasha, feeling a bit embarrassed for her detecting skills. But she told herself that it had been a hectic Yuletide, and even great detectives missed a detail now and then. The important part was that she finally knew what she needed to do. She cleared her throat to get Latouche's attention and said, "When is your next bout?"

"The finals?" said Latouche. "I dunno.

Whenever the grocer stops bragging about cauliflower, I guess." Then he added, "Any minute now."

"Crumbsy bumsy," said Sasha. "Come on, Puck. We have to move quickly." Sasha turned to run to the Wander Inn but ran instead into Papa.

An angry Papa.

A Papa with a wiggling mustache and eyebrows smooshed together into one long caterpillar, all of which was the angriest Papa that Sasha had ever seen.

CHAPTER 10

"I can explain," said Sasha.

"What can you explain?" said Papa.

"I can explain why I left the stand unattended."

"Is that why you think I'm angry? Didn't we do this already?"

"Yes?" said Sasha. Then she said, "No."

Papa didn't respond. His arms were crossed.

"Okay, maybe you're still upset that I left Puck in the stand and lost a bunch of money because he doesn't know what money is."

Papa didn't say anything.

"Okay, fine," said Sasha. "I'm sorry I dis-obeyed you...twice."

Sasha was certain that was the answer. But Papa was still waiting.

"What, then?" said Sasha.

"You lied to me."

"Did I?"

"You said you'd stay at the stand. Your word, Sasha Bebbin, is your bond."

Sasha sighed. She looked around. Latouche was off preparing for his next bout. Puck stood beside her but stared at the ground, pretending that something in the dirt was extremely interesting.

She said, "I'm sorry, Papa."

Papa's caterpillar eyebrow separated back into two smaller caterpillars, which was the right number for them to be.

"Come on," he said, turning back toward the market. "Let's go back." Papa was never mad for very long.

Sasha waved for Puck to come closer. She whispered, "You have to run to the inn to get Uncle Nestor to come watch Latouche in his last bout, okay?"

Puck nodded vigorously.

"This is an important mission, okay?"

Puck nodded harder.

"No getting distracted by a butterfly or something."

Puck's eyes narrowed at the insult. It was obvious that he prided himself on completing missions before he ran off to play with butterflies.

He scampered off on all fours, faster than any dog Sasha had ever seen. He darted between the legs of festivalgoers and disappeared.

Sasha followed Papa and hoped that this time, on her last chance, she would succeed. That was the moment she looked over at the knights' field and noticed five things all at once:

1. The greengrocer standing on his soapbox, waving celery at the crowd to show off the leafy fronds.

2. Belfort playing slap hands with the children gathered around him.

3. The lamplighter Gorch and the baron Vadim Gentry lurking around Belfort's horse, looking very suspicious.

4. Latouche slouched beside a cart, where an old traveler was roasting chickpeas and red peppers.

5. The brother and sister hedge knights, Coral and Sage, sitting in the stands, cracking walnuts with their sword hilts and bickering.

It all came together at once.

A plan.

An unlikely plan.

"Wait!" she said.

Papa stopped and turned around.

"I'm sorry I disobeyed, Papa. And I'm sorry I broke my word."

"It's okay," said Papa.

"But," said Sasha.

"No buts," said Papa.

"But it is extremely important that I go—right now—to help someone. I know you need me at the market. I know you want us to have a special Yuletide because we might lose the house. And I know Mom won't be back in time. I know I disappointed you. But I'm telling the truth. It's very important."

Papa's eyebrows turned, once again, into one long caterpillar. But this time it was a sad, downcast caterpillar. Papa was always worrying for Sasha.

"Of course," he said. He smiled as best he could.

Sasha said, "Thank you. I'll be back as soon as I can. Thank you."

And she ran toward the tournament grounds as fast as she could, hoping she wasn't too late.

CHAPTER 11

Sasha was too late.

Just as she arrived at the tournament grounds, the greengrocer finished his lettuce demonstration and shouted, "Get your discount spinach at stall number five after the tournament. But now, the main event! Knights, to your corners!"

Sasha watched as Latouche and Belfort shook hands and then turned to go to their corners. In Belfort's corner, she noticed that Gorch was replacing the knight's jousting spear with another that looked identical. Then he snuck away with the original.

Sasha had to move quickly.

She ran up to the hedge knights, Sage and Coral, and said, "Quick, I need your help."

"What do you need?" said Coral, suddenly alert.

"Can you...I dunno...can you stop the greengrocer or something?"

"You want us to kill him?" said Sage.

"We don't do killing," said Coral.

"No," said Sasha.

"We could break a few bones, I suppose," said Sage.

"Maybe push him real hard."

"None of that," said Sasha. "Just delay him a little. Stall. I just need a little time before the tournament starts, until my friend Puck arrives."

"Ohhh! Okay," said Coral.

"Thank you," said Sasha. Then, as she ran toward Latouche, she shouted over her shoulder, "But don't hurt him!"

Sage was obviously disappointed, probably because she had had to sit through all those vegetable demonstrations. But the two gave her a salute and approached the grocer.

Sasha caught up with Latouche as he was mounting his horse. He looked glum, as if he had already lost.

"Are you ready?" she said.

"I guess," said Latouche.

He sat on his horse and sighed.

Across the muddy field, Belfort looked like a giant. His armor glistened. He sat up straight. He didn't look at all afraid.

"You know," said Sasha. "I think you were wrong before, at the inn, when you said Belfort was brave because he wasn't afraid of anything."

"Okay," said Latouche.

"You don't think so?"

"I think you're a kid, and I have no idea what you're talking about. Anyway, I'm kind of busy here."

Over at the grocer's box, Sage and Coral approached. Coral smiled and tossed his coin purse up and down. He said, "My good man, I've heard about your fruits and vegetables all day, and I'd like to purchase ten—no twenty—bushels of lovely lemons."

The greengrocer's eyes grew wide with the happy thought of selling so many lemons. "Yes, yes, of course!"

"Of course what?" said Sage, who stepped forward with her arms crossed. The two knights towered over the greengrocer, even though he was standing on a box.

"Lemons, of course," said the grocer.

"But he didn't say any old lemons, did he?" said Sage.

"I'm sure he meant it," said Coral, turning to his sister.

"You're sure? How would you know?" said Sage.

The grocer was a bit confused as the sibling knights began to bicker.

"Look at him," said Coral. "Look at his face. That's an honest face."

Sage looked at the grocer and squinted. The grocer stood up straight and tried to look respectable.

"Sorry," said Sage. "Don't see it."

"That's just rude," said Coral. He turned to the grocer. "Go on, my good man. Tell her."

"Um..." For once the greengrocer did not know what to say. "Tell her what?"

"That your lemons aren't any old lemons."

"Oh! They're surely not!"

"But are they *lovely* lemons?" said Sage.

The grocer nodded.

"Say it, then," said Sage.

"Lovely lemons," said the grocer. "We've got the loveliest lemons. Lovely, lovely lemons."

"That's good," said Sage, "cause my foolish brother here forgets to ask every time, and we need lovely lemons if we're going to make our lovely lemon liniment."

"Well, sister, you can be certain now," said Coral. "My good man here will declare once and for all that his lemons are lovely lemons for making lovely lemon liniment. Then we'll pay him this big bag of gold and be on our way. Okay?"

"Fine," said Sage.

Both knights turned toward the greengrocer and waited. The old man shifted a bit on the box and cleared his throat.

"Go ahead," said Sage.

The grocer made a nervous chuckle. "Yes. Well, I am happy to declare that my lemons are lovely lemons for making lovely lemon liniminamin." His tongue seemed to shrivel on the last word, and he mumbled a noise that sounded like a lemon tumbling down a hallway.

Sage didn't say anything. Her right eyebrow raised slowly.

The grocer tried again.

"Lovely lemon liminim."

"We don't make liminim, sir," said Coral.

"Lovely lemon liminimin. Lovely lim liminent. Lovelem liminint."

The grocer's attempts were getting further and further from the phrase as his mouth seemed to fill with more and more marbles. Coral looked around and spied that dirt-covered boy,

Puck, dressed in far too little clothing for the wintertime, leading the burly innkeeper by the arm. The two squeezed into the front row to watch the tournament.

"Very well," said Coral, putting the coin purse back on his belt. "I'm sorry to have bothered you, my good man."

Sage made a curt nod. They both gave the disappointed grocer a salute and walked off. In the distance, Sasha watched as they walked away, and the grocer resumed his job of starting the tournament.

She grabbed Latouche's boot so that he would pay attention and said, "Listen. Look at that knight across the way."

"I see him," said Latouche, looking at Belfort. "He's huge."

"He's huge, and I can guarantee that he's scared. Even though you're half his size and

much, *much* weaker."

"Gee, thanks."

"But he's still scared, because he knows that anything can go wrong. He knows there are unknown dangers in this world that we can never see coming. And he knows if something happened to him, he wouldn't see his daughter again. So he's right to be scared."

The grocer called for the knights. "Ready!"

The crowd stood up.

Latouche nudged his boot away from Sasha.

Sasha said, "Do you see what I mean? Belfort isn't brave because he has no fear. He's brave because he faces his fear and does what he needs to do anyway."

The grocer shouted, "Get set!"

Sasha said, "Face your fear."

Latouche scoffed. "If you say so."

"CHARGE!" called the grocer.

Belfort tilted forward, and his warhorse began to gallop. Latouche did the same.

The crowd roared.

Sasha cringed as she watched. The odds weren't good for Latouche. The great Daytime Knight Belfort rode at full speed. But when he lowered his jousting spear, everyone could see that something was wrong. The top half of the wooden spear had been cut. It broke off as he rode and dangled by a splinter. The crowd gasped.

"Gorch," said Sasha under her breath. It was clear now how Baron Gentry planned to win. He must have wagered that Belfort would lose, so he had the lamplighter cut the knight's spear.

In the seconds before the two soldiers met, Belfort made a quick decision. As soon as he saw his broken spear, he shrugged and dropped it.

"No!" said Coral.

"He's unarmed," said Sage.

The crowd and Sasha and everybody held their breath for the moment of impact.

Belfort rode toward Latouche holding nothing.

Latouche thrust his spear forward.

Belfort turned sideways and leaned forward to let it hit his armored shoulder pad. The spear exploded into a thousand pieces, but Belfort remained seated. It was as if Latouche had run into a wall. The force of it knocked Latouche backward off his horse.

Latouche hit the mud. His horse rode on.

Belfort continued to the other side.

Belfort had won.

Latouche had lost. So had Vadim Gentry. As soon as the joust was over, the baron skulked out of the festival, shouting at Gorch.

Sasha had no idea what to do.

The crowd rushed onto the field to celebrate.
Several boys tried to lift Belfort onto their
shoulders but couldn't. The grocer jumped up
and down on his box yelling, "What a match!
Hail to the heroes! Two great warriors. Everything thirteen percent off!"

Puck and Nestor ran to Latouche and helped

him up. Sasha joined them. "Are you okay?" she said.

Latouche looked a little dazed. Nestor clapped him on the shoulder and said, "My boy, what a show! You really gave that mountain a wallop!"

Latouche smiled. He said, "That was terrifying."

"'Course it was," said Nestor, chuckling. "Only a doofus would look at that blond gorilla and be unafraid. It shows smarts to be afraid. But you did it anyway."

Uncle Nestor slapped him on the back again. For the first time all day, Sasha saw a smile—a real smile—on Latouche's face. She only had one part left in her plan. She said, "That was real bravery, wouldn't you say, Uncle Nestor?"

"Sure would."

"And you could probably tell the story for years."

"Sure will."

Uncle Nestor re-created the crash by gesturing with one hand like a galloping horse and hitting it smack into the other. Then he laughed. Puck did it as well. He punched one hand into the other and made it fly backward. He howled with laughter and rolled in the snow.

"Well, if it's a great tale of bravery," said Sasha, "then maybe it should go up on your wall."

Latouche tensed. Uncle Nestor had been laughing so hard that he had to wipe a tear from his eye. Then he said, "Aye. You're right. Come by the inn, and we'll see if Mina would be willing to paint our Latouche, the man who faced down a mountain."

"Really?" said Latouche.

Uncle Nestor put his arm around him and said, "Merry Yuletide, kid."

Puck made a happy grunting sound and

hugged Sasha's leg. Sasha was so happy she laughed and cried at the same time.

As she and Puck walked back to Papa's honey mull cider stand, Sasha patted Puck on the head and said, "Merry Yuletide, Puck."

Somehow, even with all the trouble, even though she didn't have any gifts to give or to get, Sasha had never been merrier.

Her mother was still a thousand miles away, but Sasha knew she was safe. And that was the only gift she wanted.

Besides, she had Papa.

And she had Puck, whatever he was.

And she had saved the Juicy Gizzard once again.

100 Years of
Albert Whitman & Company

1919–2019

Albert Whitman & Company encompasses all ages and reading levels, including board books, picture books, early readers, chapter books, middle grade, and YA

Present

2017

The Boxcar Children celebrates its 75th anniversary and the second Boxcar Children movie, *Surprise Island*, is scheduled to be released

The first Boxcar Children movie is released

2014

2008

John Quattrocchi and employee Pat McPartland buy Albert Whitman & Company, continuing the tradition of keeping it independently owned and operated

Losing Uncle Tim, a book about the AIDS crisis, wins the first-ever Lambda Literary Award in the Children's/YA category

1989

1970

The first Albert Whitman issues book, *How Do I Feel?* by Norma Simon, is published

Three states boycott the company after it publishes *Fun for Chris*, a book about integration

1956

1942

The Boxcar Children is published

Pecos Bill: The Greatest Cowboy of All Time wins a Newbery Honor Award

1938

3 1170 01104 4710

1919

Albert Whitman & Company is started

Albert Whitman begins his career in publishing

Early 1900s

Celebrate with us in 2019!
Find out more at www.albertwhitman.com.